**"Go then, starve to death," he shouted.
"I never wanted you anyway."**

Daniel slipped the choke-chain off Lady's neck
and ran as fast as he could across the soft earth.
Looking back, he saw Lady creeping on her belly
down a corn row, watching him distrustfully over
her shoulder. With her tail curled under between
her legs, she dashed for the woods at the far
end of the field. In a moment Daniel lost sight
of her as she plunged into the creek bed. He
followed her with a sick feeling in his stomach
and tears dripping from his chin. In the distance
he could see Lady where she sat at the edge of
the woods, watching him. He watched back until
she fled into the brush. She was gone for good
now, he was sure.

"Uncommonly effective."   *Kirkus Reviews*

The
Comeback Dog

The Comeback Dog

Jane Resh Thomas

drawings by
Troy Howell

A BANTAM SKYLARK BOOK®
TORONTO • NEW YORK • LONDON • SYDNEY • AUCKLAND

RL 5, 008-011

THE COMEBACK DOG

A Bantam Book / published by arrangement with
Houghton Mifflin Co./Clarion Books

PRINTING HISTORY

Clarion edition published Spring 1981

Bantam Skylark edition / February 1983
2nd printing . . . . February 1983
3rd printing . . . . April 1984

ISBN 0-553-15192-4

Published simultaneously in the United States and Canada

Bantam Books are published by Bantam Books, Inc. Its trademark, consisting of the words "Bantam Books" and the por-
trayal of a rooster, is Registered in U.S. Patent and Trademark
Office and in other countries. Marca Registrada. Bantam
Books, Inc., 666 Fifth Avenue, New York, New York 10103.

PRINTED IN THE UNITED STATES OF AMERICA

CW   12   11   10   9   8   7   6   5

For Jason Thomas
(Kitty loves him)—J.R.T

For Mother—T.H.

One

"I don't want another dog! I hate dogs!" Daniel shouted. "I wish I'd never laid eyes on Captain!"

"Daniel, you've done nothing but mope around this house since Captain died," said his mother. "A month is long enough."

The canary at the window had stopped singing. Daniel put his head down on the table and played with his fork. "You and Pa don't even care," he said.

"Of course we care," said his mother. She removed the hairpin from the knot at the back of her neck, twisted her lank hair several turns tighter, and jabbed the pin back into place. "We knew Captain fourteen years—five years longer than we've known you. We even knew his mother when *she* was a pup."

"You act as if you don't care," repeated Daniel.

"Stop it!" his mother snapped. "I miss Captain so much I dream about him at night."

Daniel jumped up, overturning his chair. He left it there and ran out into the cold February morning. He jumped the porch steps, with his parka in one hand, and started down the walk. His teeth were chattering, but not from the cold. He jammed his fists into the parka's sleeves, ripping the lining at one armhole, and kicked a chunk of ice that sat on the walk. The ice had melted enough in yesterday's sun to freeze fast to the cement during the night, and it didn't yield when Daniel kicked it. For a minute, he thought he had broken his toe. He hoped he had. The pain in his foot helped him forget the other pain.

As his anger cooled, Daniel thought of what he had lost. It was like feeling the socket with his tongue when he'd lost a tooth, tasting the blood, stroking the tender spot, measuring the empty space.

No more Captain, who had pulled Daniel out of the water when he was a baby and had chased a frog into the pond. No more Captain, who had waited with Daniel at the school bus stop every dark winter morning and met him there every afternoon; who slept beside his bed and woke him snuffling with a cold nose at Daniel's ear.

He wandered across the farmyard, stepping in the footprints that pocked yesterday's mud. Overnight, water had frozen in the foot-shaped pools. As the ice crackled and shattered under his boots, he enjoyed the small destruction.

He picked up a fragile wafer of ice from a puddle and held it up before one eye. Through the ice, the world looked crooked and blurry. The straight lines of the windmill, with its blades going like sixty as the wind gusted, seemed broken and disconnected. Daniel could distinguish only masses of color: the dusty red of the barn and the silvery gray of the chicken coop. But the world *felt* crooked and blurry whether he was peering through ice or not. He dropped the glassy pane and watched it break into crystals at his feet.

A muddy red pickup truck with a noisy muffler pulled into the yard. Daniel looked up and nod-ded at the veterinarian who kept the cows

healthy. Usually he enjoyed watching the vet deliver a calf or give the cows their shots. Today he didn't want to talk. Doc might ask where Captain was.

Daniel scooped up a handful of stones in the driveway and limped to the roadside ditch. He liked to throw stones through the culvert that carried the ditch water under the drive, liked the *doink, doink, doink* sounds they made as they

bounced through the steel tube. He threw the first stone sidearm as hard as he could, but it made no sound. He threw a bigger rock, this one the size of an egg, but the culvert swallowed it as silently as if it were a cotton ball.

He brushed the ground clear of snow and glass that had splintered in the ditch last fall when a pair of deer hunters had shot whiskey bottles off the mailbox. Daniel had plugged the holes in the box with sticks to keep the rain out; the buckshot was still embedded in the weathered wooden post. Pa said it was a wonder the ignoramuses hadn't shot a cow or mistaken the house for a deer.

Daniel knelt in the ditch and looked down the tunnel. A dirty bundle filled the end of the culvert. As his eyes adjusted, he could see that the bundle was not rags or papers, but an animal with matted, dirty hair.

"It must be dead," he thought, "or it would have yelped when the stones hit it. That's all I need—another dead critter to bury."

Daniel sighed and looked out across the fields where he and Captain had played. He looked back at the animal blocking the culvert. If he left it there, when the snow melted, the runoff in the ditch would back up and flood the yard. He reached in and felt the cold metal and the cold stones he had thrown. The warmth of the body surprised him as he heaved it out into the ditch.

"You're a dog, and you're breathing," he said. "Just barely."

Two

The dog's eyes were open but dull. Mud clotted its white fur and made the black patches indistinct. It bared its teeth, but it didn't growl, as if moving its lips took all its strength.

Light though it was for its size, it was too big and awkward for Daniel to carry. He ran to get his rusty wagon from under the back porch and put a couple of old gunny sacks in the bottom. Powdery earth from the potatoes that had been stored in the bags sifted into the air, but the dog was so dirty and sick that Daniel thought it wouldn't notice a little dust.

He ran back to the culvert with the wagon clattering and bouncing behind him. Hurry. Load the bag of bones into the wagon. Cushion its head. Ease across the ruts the tractor had made yesterday in the sun-softened mud that now was frozen hard again. Hurry past the chicken coop. Past the corncrib.

Up the concrete ramp they went and into the barn, where Pa and Doc stood, shining a light into the mouth of a cow. Though Daniel was panting too hard to speak, the men took in everything at a glance and moved immediately to help.

"Let's get her off this cold steel so's I can look her over." Doc lifted the dog into a manger that was half full of fragrant hay. "Where'd you find her?"

"In the culvert at the end of the drive. Do you suppose she was hit by a car and crawled in there to get shelter?"

"I don't know, but she's in bad shape," said Doc. He sucked his front teeth, as he always did when he worried. Gently he flexed the dog's joints. He prodded her belly and shone the flashlight in her eyes. He listened to her chest through his stethoscope. All the while, the dog lay still and unresisting.

"Well, you got yourself a young female here," said Doc. "She looks sound. Don't think she's been in any accidents, but she's near starved to death. Run your hand along those slats."

Daniel felt the dog's ribs.

"There's no meat to pad the bone. Doubt she'll make it through the day, Dan." The vet thought for a moment, rubbing his whiskered jaw. "I'm a cow man, of course, no expert in small animals."

"She's a full-grown English setter," said Pa, sizing her up, gauging her quality. "Look at those big paws. Nice broad muzzle. Tall at the shoulder. A rangy, heavy-boned dog like this is a powerful hunter. She could have run all day. What a shame for a fine animal to come to such grief."

19

"You talk as if she was already dead," said Daniel. "Can't we do something for her?"

"She's sick to death," said Doc. "We can speed her along. I've got some stuff in my bag. One shot will put her out nice and easy. She won't feel a thing but the prick of the needle. It would be a mercy, Dan."

"No!" Daniel shouted. The stanchions creaked as all of the black-and-white cows swung their heads in unison to stare at him. "I found her," he said in a quieter voice. "I'll take care of her."

Doc looked at him over his glasses. "Okay. You can try to bring her back. Put her by the stove and try to feed her a spoonful of broth every quarter hour or so. You can try, but don't expect any miracles."

Daniel took off his parka. With Doc's help he wrapped it around the big dog and buttoned it. His father picked up the bundle in his arms, cradling it like a baby. The dog's face was white as a skull in the shadows of the hood. Her scraggly, almost hairless tail hung down like an icy rope.

"I'll finish up here on my own," said Doc. "You call me tomorrow morning early and tell me how you're doing, Daniel. Hear?"

The boy nodded. He felt thin and small, shivering there in his shirt-sleeves, surrounded by things bigger than himself—the tall, muscular men, the hulking cows, the hugeness of the barn itself. High overhead in the rafters, a pigeon flapped. The cows chewed their hay, noisy and wide-eyed, as if a full mouth were all the world to them. With the same oblivious gaze, they would stare at the wall or whisk flies with their tails or step unawares on a kitten.

Daniel opened the door for his father. "Come on, dog," he said. "You're not dead yet."

Three

Crossing the yard they leaned against the wind. Daniel's thin shirt billowed, baring his chest to the cold, but he kept his hand like a lifeline on the dog's flank. He noticed how smoothly his father moved and how easily the big dog lay in his arms.

"Guess we got too smug and comfortable yesterday in that thaw," said Daniel's father, glancing at the heaped gray clouds at the end of the sky. "Winter's going to remind us who's boss.

He'll pick us up and shake us and set us down again when he's good and ready."

"A north wind like this swoops right through the culvert," said Daniel. "She wouldn't have lasted much longer, that dog."

"We'll put her by the stove and see what happens."

They avoided the broken board in the creaky steps.

"You were going to fix that Thursday, and here it is Saturday morning already," Daniel's father said. "Those steps have got to be fixed before something worse than a board gets broken, and I don't have the time."

"They'll be right when you come back to the house," said Daniel.

As the kitchen door slammed behind them, his mother looked up from the dishes she was washing and smiled. "Well, I see you came back," she said. "Who's that wearing your parka?"

Daniel's father laid the dog gently on the floor. "She's all yours, Son. I'll be in the barn," he said.

Daniel pushed back the hood of the parka. "I'll

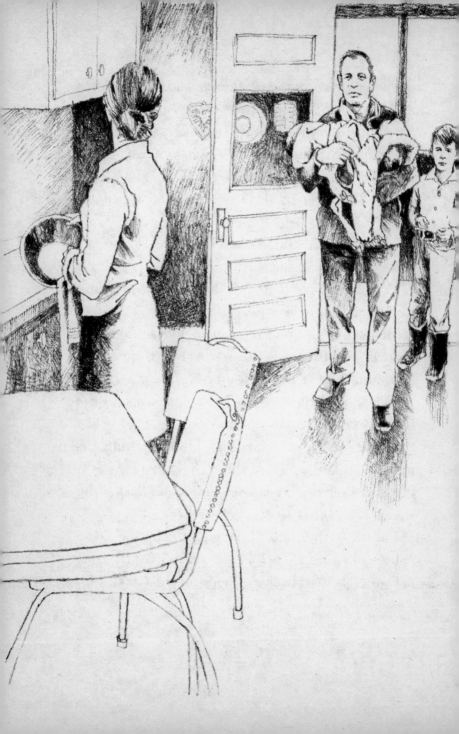

need some rags, Mama. She's sick, but Doc says there's always hope."

His mother shook the soapsuds on her hands into the sink and reached for the rag bag that hung on a hook in the pantry. "Lord knows we've got plenty of rags. I can hardly tell the difference between the rags and the clothes we're wearing." She sighed. "We'll put her by the wood stove."

"I'm afraid she'll stink."

"I've smelled worse than wet dog," his mother said. "We can always air the house."

"Doc said to give her a little broth every fifteen minutes."

"Then I'll put a tough old hen on to stew, and we'll have creamed chicken and peas for supper." She hugged the boy. "I'm glad for your kind heart, Daniel."

Arranging the faded rags behind the stove in the dining room, between the woodbox and the couch, the boy noticed that the wood was nearly gone. On such bitter windy days, the oil furnace made too little heat, and the stove gobbled logs faster than Daniel could chop them and carry them in.

As he moved the dog to her bed, she half opened her eyes, but they looked dull and blind. He and his mother dried the dog's coat with towels. She groaned, as if the gentlest touch hurt her bones.

"What's her name?" said Mama.

"I'm afraid to name her."

"How about something contrary, like Fang? Or Wolf? Maybe we can scare off death with a joke," said his mother.

"Lady," said Daniel. "That's what I'm going to call her."

"All right, then. Lady she is."

Four

When the broth was ready, Daniel filled a
medicine dropper and emptied it inside the dog's
cheek. Twice the broth dribbled out of her muzzle, but she swallowed the third dropperful.

"Let her rest now," said Mama. "More than a
few drops at a time might make her throw up.
Then she'd be worse off than she was without
us."

As Daniel knelt beside the dog, he thought of

27

Captain. He jumped up before the tears could get a good start.

"Your parka's in the washing machine," said Mama. "It was smeared with mud inside and out. Wear this for now."

She helped him into his father's old flannel-lined denim jacket. He let her put one hand on the back of his head and hug him close for a moment. She was all bone and muscle and hard spots, but her touch was gentle.

"Help her the best you can, Daniel. Then the rest is out of your hands," she said. "I see the woodbox is empty."

"Couldn't you let me off chores just once?" said Daniel.

"We've all got as much work as we can do," said Mama. "Who's going to do yours, if you don't?"

"Can't I watch the dog? Just once, couldn't the rules be changed?"

"Vigilance won't cure that dog. What's going to keep her warm, or us, if we run out of wood?"

Daniel pulled away and flung himself out the back door. At the woodpile, he picked up the knotty chunk of oak that had fought the ax all winter and set it angrily on the chopping block. He chopped and chopped with all his strength, and every time the ax fell, the knot squirted off the block.

Furious, he sharpened the ax on the hand-turned grindstone Pa kept in the woodshed, wedged the knot between two logs, and chopped some more. By the time he had worn himself out, the wood lay in irregular pieces at his feet. Too tired to be angry anymore, he carried them into the house, avoiding the broken step again, and laid them on the fire. When he clanged the stove door shut, he saw the dog jump slightly.

He gave her another dropper of broth. This time she opened her eyes fully.

"Nice dog," said Daniel. His words sounded clumsy. Was he forgetting how to talk to a dog? he wondered.

He carefully smoothed her head, as his mother had caressed his own. She slept again. Daniel thought she was breathing more deeply, with less effort.

He went outside, determined to fix the back steps before Pa caught him with the job undone. He could smell the wood smoke in the air. The gray clouds were moving in rapidly; soon the blizzard would drive him indoors. He hauled out the lumber Pa had stored under the porch and

assembled his tools—a crowbar for loosening the broken board, a folding measuring stick, a saw and hammer, and a handful of two-inch nails.

He pried the old board off, carefully saving the rusted, bent nails in his jacket pocket; they could be straightened when he had more time, and used again. He measured one of the planks in the steps and marked the new lumber with a pencil. Again he measured, checking the board against the step. His father had trusted him with expensive wood; a plank sawed too short was a wasted plank.

For his fifth birthday, Daniel's father had given him a red toolbox filled with tools fit for a man's use, not just toys that bent and broke in real work. Now, four years later, Daniel could saw a straight line or drive a spike straight and true. He could drill a hole or sand a board silky smooth. Last fall he had built a table for his mother's Christmas present.

He sawed the board where he had marked it, set it in its place, and drove two nails, one at each end, to attach it. Worried about Lady, he dragged a crate to the dining-room window, so he could keep an eye on her. Standing there on his tiptoes, he saw the canary hopping in its cage. The dog lay behind the stove where he had left her. She lay as still as stone. Dreading that she had stopped breathing, he went indoors but found that she was only asleep. She roused and accepted more broth.

Mama came into the dining room with an armload of folded laundry. It still smelled fresh from blowing in yesterday's warm wind.

"Don't fret—I'm keeping watch over her too," she said. "You've done just the right things for her, Daniel." She set the stack of clothes on the table and shook out a heavy red and black shirt. "Pa's jacket is so big on you, I fixed your heavy hunting shirt."

"Thanks," said Daniel, "but I'd rather wear Pa's." Daniel liked wearing his father's clothes, even though they hung on him like tents. He buttoned the comforting jacket tighter around his neck, rolled up the sleeves almost to his elbows, and went back to his work.

Snow stood in droplets on his oiled saw, but now he would soon be finished. He drove seven more nails; that made three at each end and three in the middle. Painting would have to wait for a warmer, drier day. Back to the toolshed he went again to wipe the tools with an oily cloth and hang them in their proper places on the rack. When he tried the step, he found that he had nailed it firm, without a wobble in it. He would feel good every time he stepped on that board.

Five

Daniel slept on the couch by the stove that night, while the antique, handmade clock ticked time away. He forced himself to awaken when the clock chimed the hours. Since Lady seemed more alert, he had gradually increased her ration of broth with each feeding, so that both of them could sleep for longer intervals.

At three o'clock, he woke in confusion. The fire shone through the isinglass windows in the stove door and reflected on the opposite wall in moving red shapes and shadows that terrified him. He leaped off the couch, thinking that he was in his own bed and the room was afire.

Behind the stove, Lady whined. In an instant, Daniel awoke completely, remembering where he was and why. The dog awkwardly shifted her position, raised her head, and struggled to her feet. She looked straight at Daniel with begging eyes, whining.

"What do you want? Do you need to go out?"

She whined again. Daniel carried her to the newspapers he had spread in the enclosed back porch. She made a small dark puddle on the papers. Daniel was jubilant. If her body was working, maybe the broth had helped. Maybe she was better.

"You're paper-trained," he said, "so you must have been a house dog somewhere. I wonder where you came from?"

She whined again as he carried her back to her bed.

"Yes," he said, "you can have all the broth you want. Hold on a minute, dog, and I'll warm it for you. It gets thick when it's cold."

Returning with the warm broth, he found her no longer outstretched on her side, but lying with her chin between her paws. She pushed the medicine dropper away with her nose and snuffed the side of the bowl in Daniel's hand.

"I'm not fast enough for you?" Daniel held the soup bowl under the dog's nose. She lapped and slurped the broth until she had licked the bowl dry. Then she pricked her ears and looked expectantly at Daniel.

He laughed. "For a dead dog, you sure are hungry! You're going to make a monkey out of Doc."

He pushed the lace curtains aside to look out at the blizzard that had shrieked around the house since dinner. Snow still fell so thickly that all he could see of the yard lamp was a glowing swirl. The wind had dropped, and the snow was coming down in big soft flakes. Spruce trees and

hedges planted as windbreaks partially protected the farmyard. Elsewhere, snowdrifts had closed country roads by now, buried fences and mail-boxes, and filled ditches.

Daniel thought with satisfaction—as if he had planned and organized the snowstorm himself—that the school bus would be kept away from his house for several days. That would be long enough for him to get Lady back on her feet.

He imagined himself teaching her to herd the cows as Captain used to do, running across the meadow on cold spring mornings with his breath visible in gusts. In his mind, Daniel saw her play-ing Captain's old games. She would bring him sticks to throw and bark at him until he cooper-ated. She would sleep under his covers on winter nights and lie with her chin on his foot while he did his homework.

Then he looked at the skinny dog that lay by the stove, already sleeping again. Her big feet and starved legs were like clubs. Her coat was so sparse he could see her knobby spine and her ribs.

Even if she lives, he thought, she may not stay here. I didn't want a new dog. Maybe she doesn't want a new boy. Maybe she'll go back home where she belongs.

Six

The snow blocked the road to school for three days. By the time the county plow cleared a path for the milk truck and the mail on Tuesday afternoon, Daniel thought he had shoveled a ton of snow.

He had dug out the mailbox and mounted a red bandanna on a long stick above it so the snowplow wouldn't shear off the post. The plow buried the mailbox again, bandanna and all. Daniel dug it out once more.

He had helped his parents clear the driveway and barnyard and had made paths from the house to the outbuildings. Where the drifts were deepest, the snow was piled higher than his head on both sides of the path. He wanted to dig a hideout, but he had no time for play.

Every morning, even before he dressed, Daniel had put out fresh water and food for Lady. "You'll have to take care of yourself, dog," he said. "I'm lucky they'll give me time off to eat." Every evening her dishes were empty.

On Wednesday, Daniel and his father came into the house together for breakfast. They had fed and watered the chickens, gathered the eggs, and milked the cows before the sun rose. Manure from the barn and chicken coop stuck to their boots, so they changed into house shoes on the porch.

Daniel gave the wire basket full of eggs to his mother, who would keep a few, sort the others for size and freshness, and sell them at the cross-roads store.

"Thank you, Daniel," she said. "The chickens are laying better since I changed their mash."

She handed Daniel a jar of homemade applesauce and a serving spoon. He dished up the sauce as she spooned fried potatoes and side pork from the iron skillet onto three large plates. Daniel's mouth watered as they carried the plates into the dining room, where Pa was opening the mail and listening to the radio.

"They say the roads are open. School today," said Pa.

"Did you hear that, dog? School will be a vacation from all this work." Daniel dropped down on his knees beside the stove, where Lady was watching them out of the corner of her eye, her ears laid back.

As he lunged happily toward her, Lady bared her teeth and snarled. She jumped to her feet and crawled under the couch. She cowered in the darkest corner, shivering and watchful.

"What's the matter with her?" said Daniel.

"Something more than starvation ails that

dog," said Mama, pouring two cups of steaming coffee and a mug of cocoa for Daniel.

"Looks like she's taken some beatings from somebody," said Pa. "Sometimes people's meanness ruins dogs. She may never be any good."

"I'll train her," said Daniel. "Now that we've caught up on the work, I'll take her outdoors after school. I'll throw sticks for her."

"You'd better put her on a leash," said Pa. "If you don't control her until this place seems like home, she'll run."

In the weeks that followed, Lady looked healthier every day. With Doc's advice, Daniel gradually changed her diet from liquids to bland foods to meat. After her appetite returned, she was constantly hungry. The weight she gained was visible. Her eyes were bright, and her coat began to shine.

When Daniel thought no one was looking, he tried to train her. He dragged her out from her place under the couch and held her head between his knees while he stroked her silky hair.

44

He forced her to lie under the table while he did his homework, and jabbed her with the toe of his boot when she inched away. He shut her in his room at night and held her in his bed with his arm locked around her neck. He even tried to make her lick his hand.

But inevitably his grip relaxed when he fell asleep. In the morning, he found her in the closet, squeezed under the low shelf, or far under the bed, with fluffs of dust caught in her whiskers and eyebrows.

Lady never snarled at Daniel again, but she wouldn't wag her tail either. She merely submitted.

One day after school, when Daniel found her under the couch as usual, he lost all patience. As he grabbed her hair and yanked at her, she yelped and whined.

"What's the matter with you?" he said. "I'm the one who fed you when you were half dead."

"You can't squeeze blood out of a turnip, Daniel," said his mother quietly at the kitchen door.

"What's that supposed to mean?"

"You can't get love by force, if she's not willing."

Daniel let Lady go, and she crawled back under the couch.

"She's not a bit like Captain," he said. "He followed me everywhere. I had to lock him up to get rid of him."

His mother knelt beside him and put her arm around him. "Every dog has ways of its own," she said.

"She let me touch her when she was sick because she couldn't get away." He wiped his eyes on his flannel sleeve. "Now she won't come near me."

His mother nodded.

"Maybe she thought I didn't want another dog. Maybe it's my fault she doesn't like me."

His mother patted his head.

"She's worse than nothing!" Daniel cried. "I wish she had died that first day. I wish I'd never found her!"

Seven

The last week of March brought robins and weather so warm the family worked outdoors without jackets. The remaining snow melted suddenly. The runoff overflowed the creek and flooded the fields near the house. Within a few days, the water receded, and warm winds and sun dried the ground.

After the chores were done and breakfast was over on Saturday morning, Daniel's father said, "Take this morning off, Daniel. You and Lady can check all the fences around the west meadow, while I muck out the barn."

"I'd rather walk fences than shovel manure any day," said Daniel.

His father watched as the boy pulled Lady from under the couch, fastened the choke-chain around her neck, and snapped the leash onto the ring. The chain ran through a larger ring, like a slip knot, so that tension on the leash would tighten the chain around the dog's neck.

Daniel pulled on the leash. Lady sat back, stubbornly stiffened her front legs, and leaned in the opposite direction. Daniel jerked the leash. She coughed and gagged as the chain pinched her windpipe.

"A choke-chain can be a brutal thing, Daniel," said his father, in a voice so soft it was almost a whisper.

"Oh, you know I won't hurt the dumb dog,"

Daniel said. He put his head down so his father couldn't see the redness in his hot cheeks as he pushed Lady across the dining room, through the kitchen, and out the back door.

They walked side by side across the yard, past the windmill and the chicken coop, but they were not companions. Lady skulked along, close to the ground, watching Daniel, leaning as far as she could against the leash.

"You don't trust me one bit, do you, dog?" Daniel said. "I saved you, but now you can't wait for the thinnest chance to get away."

As they crossed the lane between the farmyard and the fields, Daniel picked up a short stick, thinking Lady might chase it. She shied away so fearfully she fell over on her side, whimpering, and pawing at the ground as if she wished she could crawl into the earth. She rolled on her back, with her feet in the air in a gesture of surrender.

Furious, Daniel threw the stick with all his strength over last year's chopped-off cornstalks.

He slipped the choke-chain off Lady's neck and ran as fast as he could across the soft earth. Looking back, he saw Lady creeping on her belly down a corn row, watching him distrustfully over her shoulder.

"Go, then! Starve to death!" he shouted. "I never wanted you anyway!"

When he certainly could not have caught her, even if he had tried, she bolted. With her tail curled under between her legs, she dashed for the woods at the far end of the field. In a moment, Daniel lost sight of her as she plunged into the creek bed, still filled with cottony morning fog.

The creek divided the cornfield, with banks that were now two or three feet above the water. As Daniel approached it, with a sick feeling in his stomach and tears dripping from his chin, he bent automatically to pick up a field stone. Although he and his father had carried off wagon-loads of rocks from that field, every spring the frost had heaved up more.

Looking down, he noticed the claw of a dead crayfish and nearby another. The claws were everywhere, no longer the clay-green color of the living animal, but blue as could be, with red edges on the pincers.

Daniel was amazed by their number and their beauty. He knew that the flood had washed them out of the creek, but they might have been carved purposely for miniature decorations and polished by hand. Daniel imagined the multitudes of creatures living unnoticed in the creek. He filled the pockets of his windbreaker and jeans with the claws. In the distance, he could see Lady where she sat at the edge of the woods, watching him. He watched back until she fled into the brush. She was gone for good now, he was sure.

He walked back to the flower garden at the side of the house where he and his father and mother had taken turns breaking the frozen ground with a pickax, to bury Captain among the hybrid iris and rambler roses. He carefully coiled the choke-chain and the leash on the bare earth and put the crayfish in a mound beside them. Then, trying not to look toward the woods, where nothing lively moved, he walked quickly out to the barn to help his father clean the stalls.

Eight

Every day for a week Daniel pressed his cheek against the cool glass and watched from the school bus window until his eyes hurt, searching the countryside for a glimpse of white fur. Every evening, as he sat in the pool of warm lamplight at the dining-room table, trying to think about math problems, he listened for Lady, scratching like Captain to come in.

He woke up once in the middle of the night,

thinking he had heard her bark. When he opened the back door, a startled raccoon ran for cover across the moonlit yard; he knew that no coon would come near if a dog were about. Daniel picked up a stick of kindling and threw it into the darkness after the coon.

Back in bed, he shivered under blankets that had chilled while he was off fooling himself, looking for Lady. He wouldn't be tricked again by wishful thinking, he told himself. She was gone, and good riddance. He would forget her.

After that, when he caught himself with his mind wandering, looking out the bus window, searching the fields, he made himself open his books and study his homework. "There are six kinds of simple machines," he read. He shut his eyes and tried to list them without looking at the book: "the wheel, the lever, the inclined plane. . . ." But he couldn't concentrate. His thoughts returned to Lady. He worried that she might be trapped in some culvert just down the road from his house. She might have gone back to the place where somebody beat her.

Then, one chilly morning nineteen days after Lady had run off, Daniel went to the barn with his father to do the chores before school. Violins were playing a love song on the radio that ran all day to soothe the cows so they would give more milk.

As the door creaked open, a shaft of sunshine lit a pile of hay in the corner, and there crouched Lady. Daniel saw that her nose and lips and even one eyelid bristled with broken white needles.

"Look at her!" said Daniel. "What a mess."

"She's tangled with a porcupine," said Pa. When he reached for her, she snarled. "She wants nothing to do with me."

"She can cure herself then," said Daniel. He pulled down the bill of the green and yellow cap the machinery dealer had given him, until it all but covered his eyes.

"For heaven's sake, Daniel, what do you want of that dog?" said Pa. "You've been grieving for nearly three weeks because she ran away. Now you're mad because she's come back."

Lady struggled to her feet and limped to

Daniel's side. She raised her ragamuffin head high, erect and stately as a show dog, looking at him imploringly with her uninjured eye.

Daniel turned his back on her and kicked a pail so hard it bounced and banged halfway across the barn, rolled into the straw, and bumped a cow in the shins. The cow jumped back, surprisingly nimble, but with her head fastened in the stanchion, she couldn't go far. The whole herd shifted, frightened by the noise.

"Daniel, stop and look at yourself." Pa rarely spoke so sharply. "No matter how you feel, I won't have you disturbing the cows."

"I didn't mean to kick it so hard," said Daniel.

As he retrieved the bucket and patted the insulted cow on the nose, Lady followed him. He tried not to look at her, but she whined and nudged him and stood on his foot.

"It's now or never, son," said Pa. "She's yours if you want her."

Tears spilled down Daniel's cheeks. He knelt beside her, put his arms around her shoulders, and whispered in her ear, "Of course I'll help."

"Hold on, and I'll get the pliers," said Pa.

Daniel sat on a crate with the dog's head in his lap. "You're a good dog," he whispered, as he gripped the porcupine quills close to the skin with the narrow-nosed pliers. Then he drew them out one by one. "Good Lady. We're halfway done."

Her whole face was swollen and infected. She trembled in his lap, moaning and watching his every move with her good eye, but she sat still. When Daniel had pulled out all of the quills, first from her eyelid and then from her muzzle, he took a deep, shuddering breath. His hands were shaking.

"Look her over carefully," said Pa. "Your grandfather claimed that porcupine needles move into an animal's body. He said they might kill a bear if they lodged in a place the bear couldn't reach."

Together Daniel and Pa gently made the dog lie down. She lay patiently still as they combed through her hair with their fingers and inspected every part of her body.

"Look at her paws," said Daniel. "Sores all over the pads of her feet."

"She must have tried to clean her face and pierced her paws with the needles," said Pa, "but she could pull those out with her teeth."

"I don't know how she could walk," said Daniel.

The door swung open as Mama came into the barn, hugging herself in a heavy knitted sweater. "What's happened? Breakfast is getting cold," she said, squinting in the dim light of the barn. "Why, it's Lady!"

"She's come back," said Daniel.

His mother saw the porcupine needles at Daniel's feet and the pliers in his hand and Lady's hurt face. "I begin to doubt that dog's sense," she said. "Bring the old pincushion up to the house and we'll put some salve on her face."

Lady wouldn't let Pa pick her up but cringed and clung to Daniel.

"It's a good thing we weren't quick to get rid of her bed," said Mama.

"Look how bedraggled she is," said Daniel.

"We'll have to start dang near fresh, fattening her up again. What a pain in the neck you are, dog."

He turned away from her and walked into the morning sunshine. "I can't carry you," he said, "and I got rid of the leash. You'll have to make it on your own power."

Slowly Lady followed the boy through the barn door and limped across the yard. The windmill swung and squeaked in the rising breeze. The tulips Daniel had planted along the sidewalk last fall had broken through the ground, and the yellow cups bobbed on stiff stems. The air was alive with a robin's song.

Footsore and stiff and muddy as on the day Daniel had first seen her, the dog wagged her tail and licked his hand.

Overcome by the morning, he took off his cap and skimmed it into the branches of the oak he climbed in summer. "Lady's come back on her own," he said to the birds.

He bent and kissed the dog on her hot, dry nose. "Maybe this time," he said, "you'll stay."

About the Author

Jane Resh Thomas grew up in Kalamazoo, Michigan, where her mother taught her to love books and her father taught her to love nature. She now lives in Minneapolis, Minnesota, where she and her family enjoy both worlds—the libraries and the lakes and woods.

About the Illustrator

Troy Howell is a popular freelance illustrator whose work appears frequently in children's books and magazines. Mr. Howell received his education from Compton City College and the Art Center School of Pasadena. He now makes his home in Fredericksburg, Virginia with his wife and son.

Shop at home
for quality childrens books
and save money, too.

Now you can order books for the whole family from Bantam's latest listing of hundreds of titles including many fine children's books. *And* this special offer gives you an opportunity to purchase a Bantam book for only 50¢. Here's how:

By ordering any five books at the regular price per order, you can also choose any other single book listed (up to $4.95 value) for just 50¢. Some restrictions do apply, so for further details send for Bantam's listing of titles today.